DATE DUE			
Fe 17 1K			
Y			
Ja 24 1K			

Printed
in USA

30

What Do You Say When a Monkey Acts This Way?

Do you know . . .

A library is a magic castle with many Word Windows in it?

What is a Word Window?

If you answered, "A book," you're right.

A book is a Word Window because the words, and the pictures that tell about the words, let you look and see many things. Books are your windows to the wide, wide world around you.

CHILDRENS PRESS
HARDCOVER EDITION
ISBN 0-516-05744-8

CHILDRENS PRESS
PAPERBACK EDITION
ISBN 0-516-45744-6

Library of Congress Cataloging in Publication Data

Moncure, Jane Belk.
    What do you say when a monkey acts this way?.

    (Magic castle readers)
    Summary: Each day of the week, Little Monkey
learns appropriate behavior for a variety of
situations.
    [1. Monkeys—Fiction.   2. Behavior—Fiction]
I. Super, Terri, ill.   II. Title.   III. Series:
Moncure, Jane Belk.   Magic castle readers.
PZ7.M739Wgc   1988   [E]   87-11736
ISBN 0-89565-368-0

What Do You Say When a Monkey Acts This Way?

by Jane Belk Moncure
illustrated by Terri Super

Created by

Distributed by CHILDRENS PRESS®
Chicago, Illinois

**The Library —
A Magic Castle**

Come to the magic castle
When you are growing tall.
Rows upon rows of Word Windows
Line every single wall.
They reach up high,
As high as the sky,
And you want to open them all.
For every time you open one,
A new adventure has begun.

Jon opened a Word Window. He read . . .

On Monday Little Monkey made
mud pies. He made lots and lots
of mud pies.

When it was time for lunch,

Little Monkey ran to the table
with mud-pie hands.

What did Mama Monkey say?

"Wash your hands before you eat, Little Monkey."

And he did. He washed his hands.
That was on Monday.

On Tuesday Little Monkey pushed his sister in a swing.

He pushed her too high, and she fell out.

What did Mama Monkey say?

"Tell your sister you are sorry,
Little Monkey."

And he did. He said, "I am sorry."

Then he gave his sister a hug.
That was on Tuesday.

On Wednesday Mama Monkey made
spaghetti with cheese for lunch.

Little Monkey said, "Give me more spaghetti with cheese."

What did Mama Monkey say?

"Please say please," she said. And he did.
He said, "Please, may I have more spaghetti
with cheese?"

That was on Wednesday.

On Thursday Little Monkey had a birthday party. Each friend gave him a birthday gift.

"Hurrah!" said Little Monkey.
"Look at all my birthday gifts!"

What did Mama say? "Little Monkey, you forgot to say something!"

So Little Monkey said, "Thank-you." That was on Thursday.

On Friday Little Monkey played with his kite.

His sister said, "May I have a turn?"

"No," said Little Monkey. "This is my kite."
What did Mama say?

"Please give your sister a turn."
And he did. That was on Friday.

On Saturday Little Monkey dumped
all of his toys out of the toy box.

He played with his toys.
Then he ran outside.

What did Mama Monkey say?

"Please put your toys away."

And he did. That was on Saturday.

On Sunday Little Monkey went to
see Grandpa and Grandma Monkey.

He gave each of them a hug.
"What a big monkey," said Grandma.

They gave Little Monkey a new truck.

"Thank-you,"
said Little Monkey.

"What a big monkey," said Grandpa.

Grandpa took Little Monkey to see
his new sailboat.

"Please, may I go for a ride?" asked
Little Monkey.

"You can help me sail my boat," said Grandpa Monkey.

And Little Monkey did.

When it was time to go home, Little Monkey said, "I had a nice time. Thank-you."

Grandma gave him a cupcake.

When Little Monkey got home,
he gave his sister half of it.

Guess what Mama Monkey said?
"My, what a big monkey you are
today!"

Here are some special words that Little Monkey learned. You can read them.

"Let's share."

"I am sorry."

"Please."

"Thank-you."

33